NONNI'S MOON

Written by Julia Inserro
Illustrated by Lucy Smith

Author: Julia Inserro
Illustrator: Lucy Smith

Printed in the United States of America
First Printing, 2018
ISBN 978-1-947891-00-5

For freebies and updates on new
releases, subscribe at
www.juliainserro.com
www.lucysmithart.com

Dedicated to my three magic beans, our Daddy bean, and our own Nonni - Julia

For my lovely Dad, we miss you every day - Lucy

It was bedtime.
The moon was up and Beanie's
mom was tucking her in.

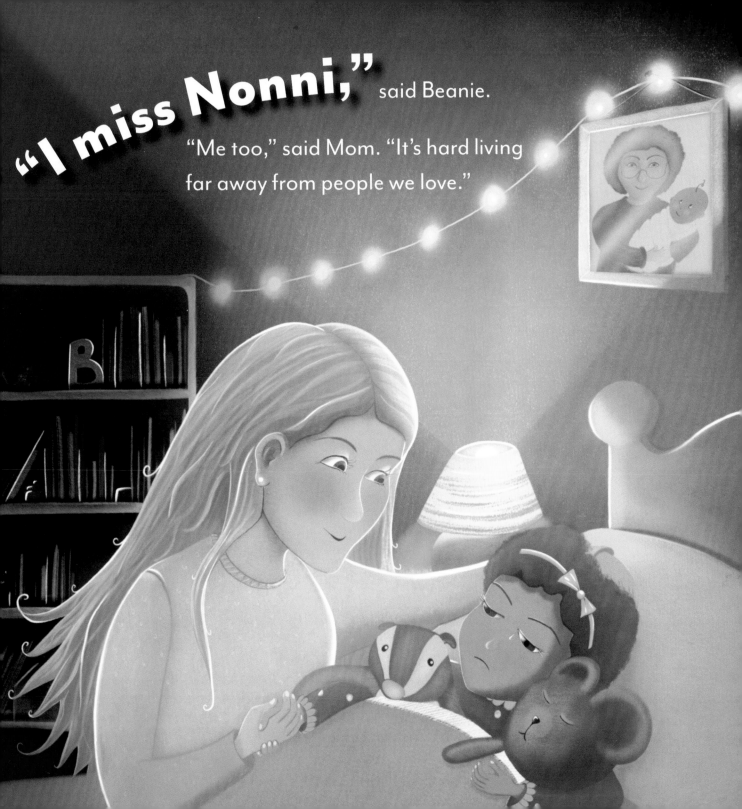

"I miss Nonni," said Beanie.

"Me too," said Mom. "It's hard living far away from people we love."

"Can we call her?" asked Beanie.

"Absolutely! Let's call her in the morning. That will be her bedtime."

"Why is it her bedtime in the morning?" Beanie asked.

"Because she lives on the other side of the world.

So when the sun is rising and waking us up, the moon is coming up for Nonni."

Giving her a kiss and a big squeeze, Mom said, "Good night, Beanie.

I love you to **pieces** and **pieces**."

In the morning, Beanie got dressed and ate breakfast as quickly as she could.

RING, RING!

"I miss you, Nonni!" Beanie said before Nonni could even say hello.

"I miss you, too, dear," laughed Nonni.

"What are you going to do today?"

"I have school with Miss Hala. We are painting."

"**That sounds fun!**"
said Nonni.

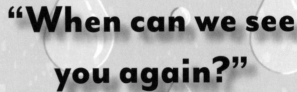

"When can we see you again?"

"Oh, it will be a while," said Nonni. "I will see you at Christmas."

"But I want to see you every day," said Beanie.

"Let's think about it. I bet there's some way we can send a message to each other every day."

She raced downstairs. "Mom, Dad, I have an idea!" she said. But before she could share it, the phone rang.

"Good morning, Beanie," Nonni said. "I thought and thought about how we could send a message every day and I think I found a solution."

"Nonni, I have an idea, too."

"The **MOON!**"

they said at the same time.

Laughing, Nonni said, "I looked up and saw the moon tonight. It was so big and bright that I couldn't stop staring. And then I thought, Beanie gets to see the **exact same moon!**"

"Yes," Beanie said.
"I saw it, too."

"So when I go to bed tonight, I can send you a message through the moon," said Nonni.

"Then later, when you see the moon, you can send a message back to me."

"That sounds great," said Beanie.
"Aren't we smart?" said Nonni.

Beanie laughed.

Beanie was **so excited** to get Nonni's message, she could barely concentrate at school.

Following dinner and books, Beanie raced upstairs to get ready for bed.

"Slow down, Beanie," said Mom. "Brush your teeth."

"But I have to get Nonni's message," said Beanie.

"I know," said Mom, "but her message will still be there after you've brushed your teeth properly."

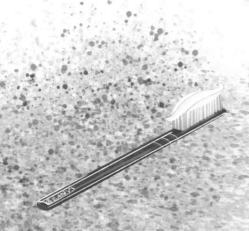

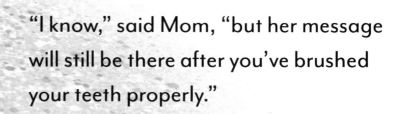

Beanie finished brushing and got into her pajamas.

"Let's look at the moon," she said as she climbed up to the window.

"Do you see a message?" asked Mom.

"I don't know," said Beanie.

"It just looks like the moon."

"How about this," suggested Mom. "Close your eyes and think of Nonni. What would she say?"

Beanie closed her eyes and sat quietly. "Can you hear her?"

"Shhh," said Beanie, **"I am listening."**

After a few minutes, Beanie smiled. "She said **she loves me,** and she misses me a lot."

"It worked!" laughed Mom.

"That's great. Now let's send her one back."

"But how do I do that?" asked Beanie.

"Well, let's close our eyes again, and imagine Nonni standing right in front of us. **What would you say?"**

Beanie thought for a moment and said, **"I love you**, and I miss you. I drew a picture of a kitty for you."

Opening her eyes, she asked, **"Is that good?"**

"That was wonderful," said Mom.

Then she gave her a kiss and a squeeze and said, "I love you to **pieces and pieces**. Nonni's going to be so excited to get your message."

Beanie fell into a deep sleep and before she knew it, she was waking up to the rising sun. Again, she raced downstairs.

"Can we call Nonni to see if she got my message?" she asked.

"Let's finish eating breakfast and then we can call her," said Mom.

RING, RING!

"Nonni, did you get my message? Did you hear that I drew you a kitty?"

Nonni laughed. "I was brushing my teeth and I saw the moon. I closed my eyes and I could hear your voice. It was wonderful. I couldn't stop smiling. And I can't wait to see the kitty picture," she said.

"It worked!"

yelled Beanie. "Let's do this again. I can't wait to go to bed tonight."

Nonni laughed. "Enjoy your day and have fun at school. Bedtime will come soon enough. I will send you another message tonight."

That day at school,
Beanie showed Miss Hala
a picture she had drawn.
**"This is Nonni's
moon,"** said Beanie.

"This is how we send messages to each other. I tell her I love
her and miss her. And she tells me she loves me, too."

"What a fabulous idea," said Miss Hala.
"Maybe I could do the same with my sister, who lives far away."

"Oh yes," said Beanie.

"All you have to do is look at the moon and close your eyes and talk.

When your sister sees the moon, if she listens very closely, **she will hear you."**

After dinner that night,
Beanie chose three books
and Daddy read all of them.

Beanie then went to get
ready for bed.

"Mom! **Dad! Come quick!**" yelled Beanie.

Mom ran into the room. "What's wrong?"

"It's Nonni's moon! **It's gone!**"
Beanie began to cry.

"What do you mean, it's gone?" asked Mom.

"Look!" said Beanie.

"It's not in the sky!"

Mom looked out the window. It was a cloudy night, and there were no stars and no moon to be seen. "What are we going to do? How can I send her a message?"

Mom smiled. "Even though you can't see it, the moon is always there. Tonight it's hiding behind some clouds, but you can still send your message, and I bet you will hear Nonni's as well."

Beanie didn't think her mom was telling the truth, but she was willing to give it a try.

"Sit here with me, and let's see if we can hear Nonni." Beanie climbed up into Mom's lap and sat quietly. "Do you hear anything?" Mom whispered.

"No," said Beanie.

"How about now?"

"Yes! I can hear her. She says she loves me, and she loved talking to us on the phone. And she said her cat Pookie did something funny."

"That's wonderful," said Mom. "See how amazing the moon is? It's just like Nonni's love. Even if you can't see it every day, it will always be with you."

"That makes me very happy."

"Me, too," said Mom. And she gave Beanie an extra tight squeeze.